THE Story

Stephanie Weaver
Illustrated by Michaela Wyse

ISBN 978-1-0980-8217-8 (paperback)
ISBN 978-1-6390-3163-4 (hardcover)
ISBN 978-1-0980-8218-5 (digital)

Christian Faith Publishing, Inc.
832 Park Avenue
Meadville, PA 16335
www.christianfaithpublishing.com

Printed in the United States of America

This book is dedicated to one of my favorite Bible teachers Miss Mel. Her ministry to kids has always been an inspiration to me!

Slamming the door behind him, Austin stomped out into the yard and kicked an empty can against the chain-link fence. There was a tightness in his chest, and his head felt like it was about to explode. Seeing the cat jumping down off the trash can, he picked up a rock and hurled it at her. Missing, the stone hit an old flowerpot as the cat squealed and darted away. He opened the side gate and headed out toward the front street. He wanted to get away from the house, and the sound of his parents' shouting. Usually when they were fighting, he would retreat to his room and watch TV to give his mind another place to go. But today there was so much built up inside him, he just wanted to run away from it all.

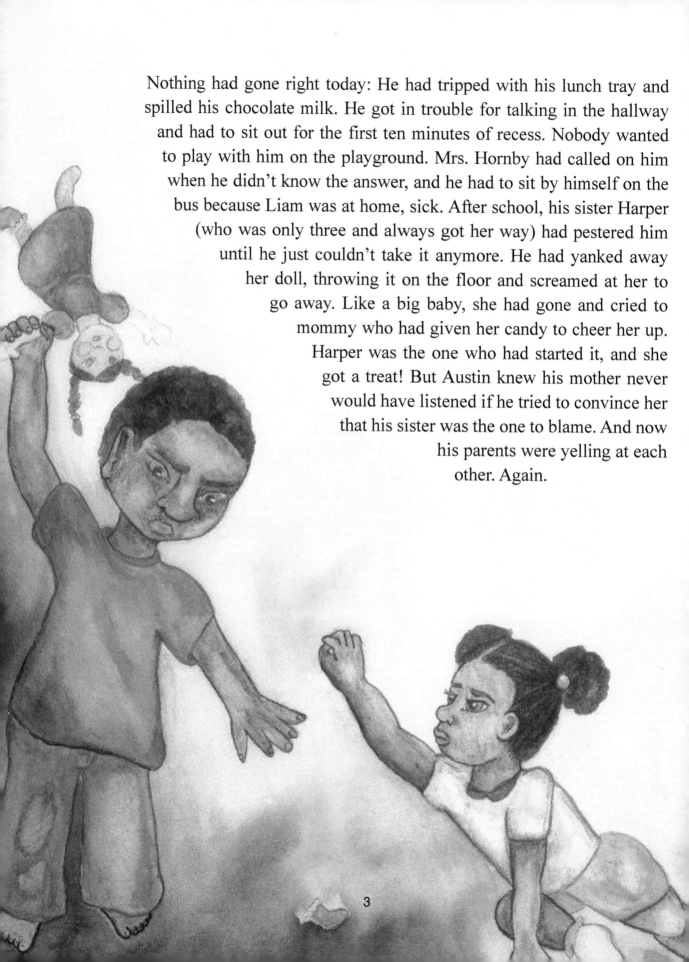

Nothing had gone right today: He had tripped with his lunch tray and spilled his chocolate milk. He got in trouble for talking in the hallway and had to sit out for the first ten minutes of recess. Nobody wanted to play with him on the playground. Mrs. Hornby had called on him when he didn't know the answer, and he had to sit by himself on the bus because Liam was at home, sick. After school, his sister Harper (who was only three and always got her way) had pestered him until he just couldn't take it anymore. He had yanked away her doll, throwing it on the floor and screamed at her to go away. Like a big baby, she had gone and cried to mommy who had given her candy to cheer her up. Harper was the one who had started it, and she got a treat! But Austin knew his mother never would have listened if he tried to convince her that his sister was the one to blame. And now his parents were yelling at each other. Again.

3

5

Life is so unfair, he thought. *But no one cares. No one ever cares.*

By now, his anger had turned to misery. There was a lump in his throat, and he didn't even try to keep the hot tears from spilling out and flowing down his cheeks. He closed his eyes tightly wishing it would all just go away.

"You okay there?" said a gentle voice.

Startled, Austin looked up and quickly brushed away his tears with the back of his hand. He looked bleakly at the lady who stood watching him from her porch. He had seen her several times before tending the flowers in front of her house or walking her dog through the neighborhood. Once, when Austin had fallen off his bike, she had come out to the street to see if he was okay. But since he wasn't used to adults paying attention to him, he had just muttered "I'm fine," and peddled quickly off again even though his leg had been badly scrapped.

Now she smiled at him warmly and said, "You look like you could use a cookie."

Then she disappeared inside the house before Austin could think how to respond. Within a few moments, the woman returned. She sat down on the front step putting a plate of cookies down next to her and motioning for Austin to join her. Biting into one of the warm chocolate-chip cookies, he sat staring shyly at his feet.

"I'm Miss Carole," she said pleasantly. "What's your name?"

"Austin," he mumbled.

"Is something troubling you, Austin?"

He hesitated. Was it safe to share his thoughts with this lady? Would she think his problems were childish or silly? He didn't even know her. But she seemed so nice. She didn't talk down at him the way grown-ups usually did. Her dark eyes were kind, and something in her voice told him that she really cared. She waited patiently for him to answer.

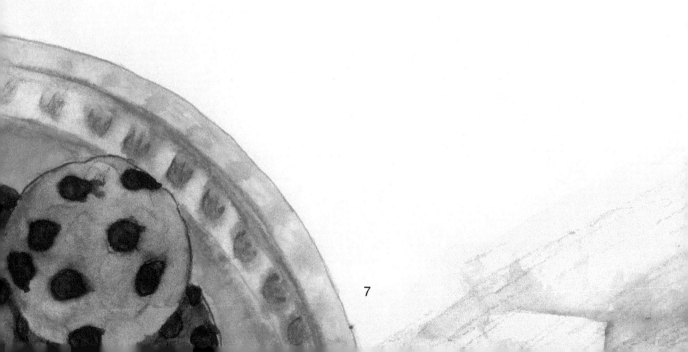

"Well," he began, "it's just that nothing ever seems to go right for me. I am always getting into trouble, and nobody likes me. My only friend at school is Liam, and even he can be mean sometimes. And he always bosses me and makes me play what he wants to play. Nobody listens to me at home, and my parents are always yelling and fighting. Sometimes I wonder if anybody loves me at all."

It felt strange to hear himself admit it out loud, and Austin wasn't quite sure why he had said it. But he realized that, that was exactly how he felt. Alone and unwanted.

Miss Carole was looking at him with a sadness in her eyes. But there was something else in her eyes too. Austin wasn't quite sure what, but it was like there was a light shining out of her that made him feel safe with her. For a long moment, she just looked at him as if she was thinking deeply about what he had said and feeling the heaviness of it with him.

Then she said tenderly, "God loves you."

8

"God?"

Austin had heard about God before. He knew his grandma went to a place called church where they talked about God. One time she had taken him with her. He had gone in a room with a bunch of other boys and girls where they had sung songs, listened to a story, and played games. But he hadn't really understood what it was all about.

"Who's God?" he asked. "And how do I know He loves me?"

He was afraid his question might sound stupid, but Miss Carole didn't laugh or make him feel like a dumb little kid.

"That's a very big question," she said. "And an important one." Then she smiled and added, "I am glad you asked."

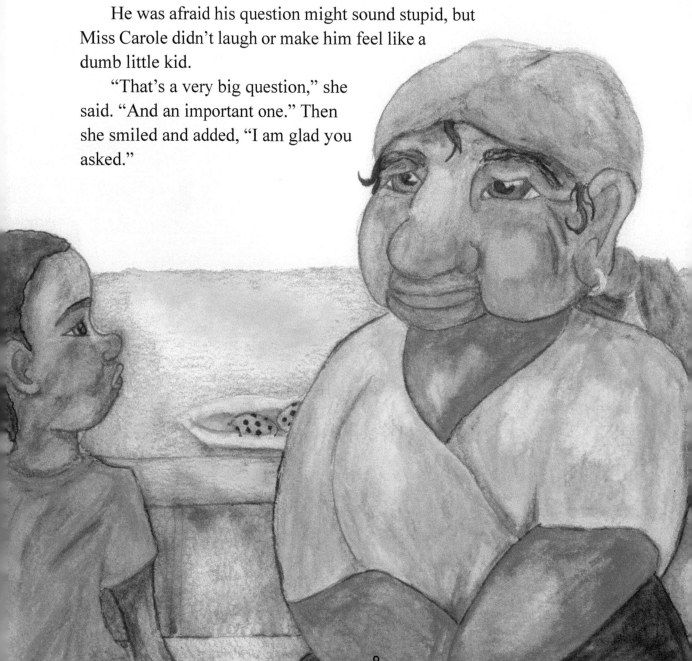

9

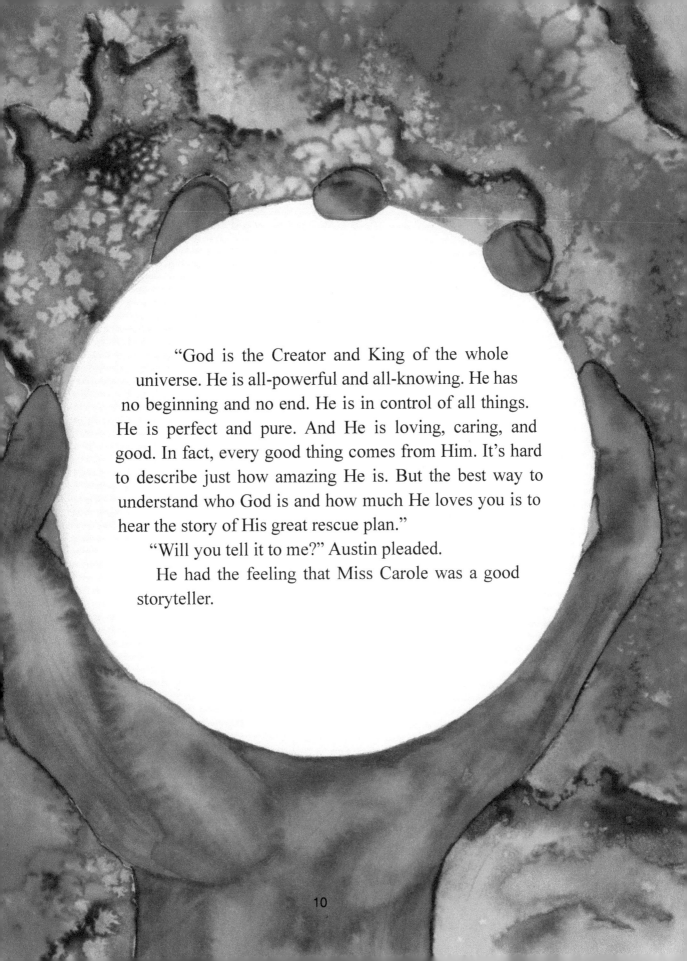

"God is the Creator and King of the whole universe. He is all-powerful and all-knowing. He has no beginning and no end. He is in control of all things. He is perfect and pure. And He is loving, caring, and good. In fact, every good thing comes from Him. It's hard to describe just how amazing He is. But the best way to understand who God is and how much He loves you is to hear the story of His great rescue plan."

"Will you tell it to me?" Austin pleaded.

He had the feeling that Miss Carole was a good storyteller.

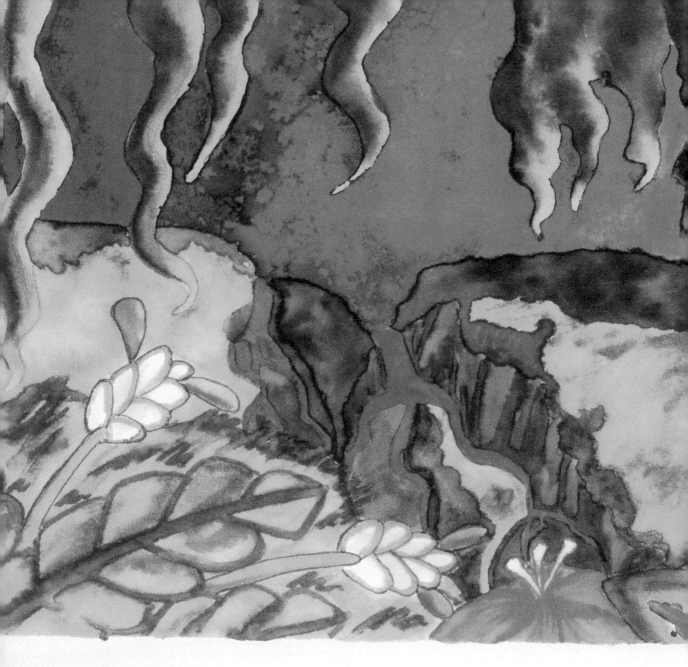

Her eyes danced as she said, "The story begins in the very beginning of time when God created the world and everything in it. It was a world full of wonder, beauty, life, and love. God created the first man and the first woman and gave them a beautiful garden to live in where they were safe and happy, and they had a very close and special relationship with Him. He delighted in them because they were his children, and they loved and adored His greatness and goodness. The only thing they knew was His love. It was a perfect paradise. But it didn't last long."

"Why not? What happened?" Austin wanted to know.

"Well, since God loved them so much, he gave them the gift of choice. He knew that it wouldn't be real love if they were forced to love him. Without choice, they would be just like robots programmed to do exactly as they're told with no will of their own. So they had the choice to love and obey God, but they also had the choice not to."

Austin thought he knew where this story was going. "Let me guess," he said, "they made the wrong choice?"

"They did," Miss Carole replied sadly. "God's enemy, Satan, came to them disguised as a serpent and lied to them about God's goodness. He got them to doubt God's love for them. They listened to the lie and decided that they wanted to make their own rules about what was right and wrong instead of trusting what God said. And so their perfect relationship with God was broken. And that's when sadness, sickness, shame, fear, pain, and death came into the world."

They sat in silence for a minute.

Then Austin asked, "Was God angry? Did he punish them?"

"God was heartbroken by their choice. And He knew that there would have to be a punishment for it. But He still loved them. He had known all along that they would make the wrong choice and disobey Him. But before He had even created them, He had already made a plan for how He would save them from the mess that their bad choice made, and how He would make a way for them to have a relationship with Him again. It was his great rescue plan."

Austin helped himself to another cookie, eagerly waiting for Miss Carole to continue.

"God promised that one day he would send a Rescuer who would destroy the serpent, all evil, and the power of death itself. He would take away all the brokenness, sickness, and pain and restore their relationship with God so that they could know Him and love Him again. So God chose a family to be His special people. He promised that He would love and protect them and asked them to love, trust, and obey Him. And He promised that the Rescuer would come from their family line. The Rescuer would make the way for all people to live in loving relationship with God again.

But it would be a long time before the Rescuer came. And in the meantime, things went from bad to worse. God's people failed to trust and obey Him over and over again. For hundreds of years, generation after generation, they continued to disobey God, turning away from Him and looking to other things to satisfy their needs and their longing for love."

"But why did God wait all those years before sending Rescuer? Why didn't He just come and take away the evil and brokenness right away?"

Miss Carole thought for a moment and then replied, "I think God wanted people to learn just how helpless they were to rescue themselves. He wanted them to see how bad their lives could get without Him so that they could appreciate how good life is with Him." She paused and then added, "And sometimes, the longer you have to wait for something, the more exciting it is when it comes."

"God's people must have been super excited about the Rescuer coming!" Austin said.

"Well, they were excited by the *idea* of a Rescuer," Miss Carole explained, "but mostly because they wanted someone to come and take away all their problems. They wanted someone who would punish the evil done against them. But what they didn't realize is that they needed a Rescuer who could also get rid of the evil in their own hearts."

"So did God send one? Did the Rescuer come?" Austin asked. Miss Carole smiled. "Yes, the Rescuer came! But not in the way anyone expected. He came as a humble servant and lived as an ordinary man. His name was Jesus. And He was God's own Son. He showed by his example what God's love looks like. He healed the sick, cared for the poor, and made friends with the people that no one else liked. He also did many miracles to show God's power and love, and to help people believe that he really was the Rescuer.

"Miracles? Like what?" Austin wondered.

"Jesus made people who were blind able to see and made people who were crippled able to walk. He walked on top of water in the middle of a storm. He used a few loaves of bread and a couple fish to make enough food to feed thousands of people. He even brought dead people back to life!"

"Wow," said Austin, "everyone must have loved Jesus!"

"Some people did," Miss Carole replied. "Some people just loved the miracles. Others were confused by Jesus and didn't know what to think of him. And some people hated him. They were jealous of him and wanted to kill him. And that's exactly what they did."

21

"Wait, what?!" Austin protested, "They can't kill the Rescuer! What kind of story is this? The hero isn't supposed to die! He's supposed to win!"

"It doesn't seem right, does it?" Miss Carole agreed. She sounded like she might cry as she said, "It was a horrible death. They whipped Him, mocked Him, spat on Him, put thorns on His head, and nailed His hands and feet to a cross of wood where He died slowly and painfully. But God had a reason for it. It was all part of the rescue plan. Just when all hope seemed lost, God surprised everyone with the most wonderful miracle of all. Three days after they killed him, God raised Jesus back to life!" Miss Carole declared, her whole face glowing and her eyes sparkling with excitement.

"Ha! I knew it couldn't end with the Rescuer dying!" Austin said. "Did He get back at the people who killed him?"

"No, He forgave them. Because that's how powerful and amazing God's love is. He forgives us for all the ways we fail to love Him. If Jesus wanted to, he could've stopped them from killing Him in the first place. But He chose to die. His death WAS the rescue plan! When Jesus died, He absorbed into himself all the evil, sadness, sickness, shame, fear, pain, and death. He chose to suffer the punishment for all the wrong choices we make. Because He knew that it was the only way to get rid of the evil in our hearts so that we can have the same kind of wonderful relationship with God that the first people had at the very beginning."

23

"What about the evil serpent?" Austin wanted to know. "Did the Rescuer destroy him?"

"In a way He did. He proved that the serpent and all the powers of evil can be defeated by the overcoming power of God. But Satan won't be destroyed once and for all until the very end of the story. One day Jesus will come back again. And this time He will come as a conquering King, banishing Satan and putting an end to evil, sickness, and sadness forever. But in the meantime, you and I are still living in the middle of the story. We can still choose to believe the serpent's lie that God doesn't really love us, or to believe in what Jesus did to show us God's amazing love. We can choose to let the evil in our hearts separate us from Him, or we can choose to ask for His forgiveness so that we're free to enjoy the kind of relationship with God that we were made to have."

Austin sat quietly, thinking about Miss Carole's story. He realized that he had all kinds of evil in his heart: lying to his parents, hating Harper and her tantrums, disobeying teachers at school, not playing fair with the other kids, and worst of all, not loving the way that he now knew God loved him. He wanted to tell God he was sorry. He thought about how Jesus had died so that people could know God's love and have a relationship with Him again.

He looked at Miss Carole. She gave him a gentle smile and a look that said she knew exactly what he was thinking. "Do you want to start a relationship with Jesus?" she asked. Austin nodded.

"Then all you have to do is tell Him that. Ask Him to forgive you, and tell Him you want to be His child. Then nothing will ever, ever be able to separate you from His perfect love."

So that's what Austin did. When he was finished, he gave Miss Carole a big smile. She smiled back, and he realized what the light was that he had noticed in her eyes before: it was God's love.

The clouds were starting to change colors with the setting sun, and Austin knew he should probably be heading home. He thanked Miss Carole for the cookies and for the story. She gave him a hug, and told him that he was welcome to come back anytime.

As Austin walked back down the sidewalk toward his house, he thought, *My parents probably never even noticed that I left.* He managed to sneak in the back door and go up to his room without having to talk to them. But he could still hear the sound of his father's angry voice, and Austin was sure that they were both still in a bad mood. He knew nothing would be different at home. Nothing would be different at school tomorrow either. Life would still be hard and unfair. He would probably still feel lonely sometimes.

But he smiled to himself knowing that one thing *had* changed. Now thanks to Miss Carole's story, He knew that Someone loved him. God loved him, and Jesus had died for him. So Austin knew that somehow everything would be okay in the end. Because that's the way God's story goes.

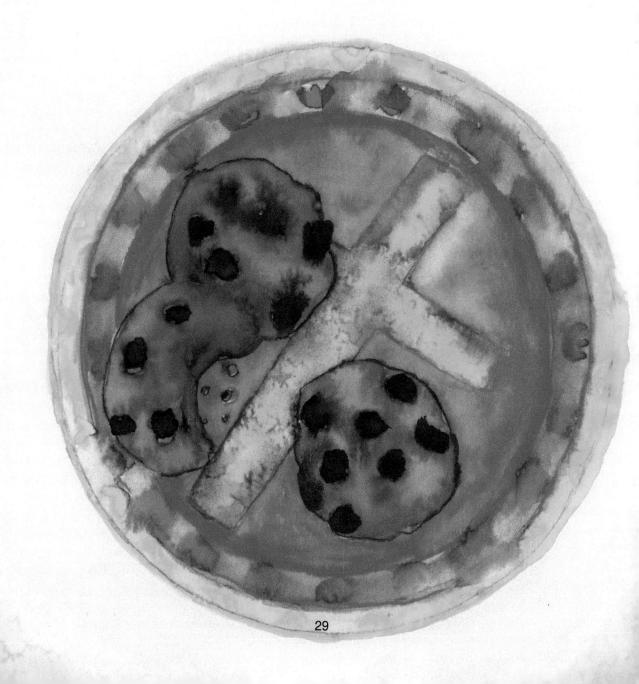

About the Author

Stephanie Weaver is a children's ministry enthusiast who is passionate about teaching kids God's Word. She is a graduate of Toccoa Falls College where she earned a bachelor's degree in counseling psychology. As the daughter of overseas missionaries born in Guatemala and raised primarily in Papua New Guinea, she is passionate about missions and feels called as a missionary to the world's largest unreached people group: KIDS!

CPSIA information can be obtained
at www.ICGtesting.com
Printed in the USA
BVHW061035291121
622781BV00010B/440

9 781098 082178